# Too Far Gone

## A novel Written By:

### S.Johnson

TOO FAR GONE

-A Novel Written by-

S.Johnson

Copyright © 2015 by Shalonda Johnson

Published by LS Johnson Publishing

Email: lsjohnsonwriting@gmail.com

First Edition

Follow on Instagram: @author_sjohnson

This novel is a work of fiction. Any resemblances to actual events, names, characters, real people, living or dead, organizations, establishments, and events are portrayed in this novel are either products of the author's imagination or are used fictitiously.

Cover design/Graphics: Donal Romano

Editor: Yadira Guzman

## Dedication

Resting in Peace my beautiful Great Grandmother Willie Mae Booker, I love you dearly. If nothing else, you taught me to always look out for myself. You made sure I knew I had come from a background of people who worked really hard. With that, I carry my head high and continue to strive for the absolute best for my family.

Alice Taylor, my heart, my grandmother; your strength has proven to me that I can do all things through Christ. You've smiled in the midst of chaos and shined a light on the darkest days. I love you and thank you.

Phyllis Theus and Earnestine Ross, two very strong women that I am thankful for every day, I love my grandmothers.

# Acknowledgments

As I sit here reflecting on my past, present, and future I must first thank God. I thank Him for giving me the hunger to serve others.

Sean and London Johnson, my two love bugs. I will do anything in my power to ensure that you two will always have unlimited resources. Without you, I would not be where I am today. You two push me to keep moving forward and inspire me every single day.

My husband, Ladellius (Ralph) Johnson, we've been through some very tough times together but the journey has built so much character. I am the happiest woman to have you by my side. An awesome supporter and provider, you've continued to show me the good in the world. God blessed me with an amazing partner in love, in the spirit and in business; you are my very best friend, I Love you.

To my mother Yolanda Givens, my rock before anything and everyone, you have supported me with everything I've decided to do. There is truly none out there like you. I love you forever.

My two little brothers Rashad Neal and Sean Keyes, this is for you to see that you can do anything you put your mind to.

My dad and step father, Sean Keyes and Rodcliff Neal thank you for contributing to my life. Dad, I thank God to have you present and looking forward to our future.

My Uncle Robert Givens, Thanks for being in my life. You have never ever left my side. Love you.

Latrice Allen, your journey inspired my own, you sparked a dead flame and I am so grateful for your mission. You gave me a chance and trusted me, thank you!

Special shout out to my cousin Jessica Pfiffer and friend Carmonique Thomas, you two have remained loyal to our friendship even though we've spent most of our time thousands of miles away from one another, our friendship remains strong. Thank you.

My team; my editor Yadira Guzman; your humility, service, and open mind have opened my eyes completely. You will reap it all. Thank you from the bottom of my heart and my Illustrator/Graphic Designer, Donal Romano, thank you for appreciating my vision and bringing it to life.

To my family and friends, all of you all have inspired me in some sort of way. I am thankful for the bits and pieces that have helped with bringing this to life. To my supporters, let this be the first of many. Thanks for trusting me to help you escape your reality for a little while; I pray you are encouraged in some way. God Bless

# Chapter 1

It's cold, but my body is warmer than usual. The smell of Sunday is in the air as my grandmother's pancakes fulfill any doubt about what today is. Every Sunday morning I take a moment to fancy the day's set up. Therefore, like every other day, I take that moment to figure out and digest what I want and need to get done. Walking down the stairs I begin to hear Grandma's routine gospel melody and the kids, Tyson and Aalyiah, screaming at one another. My big brother's radio is blasting in his attempt to zone out the rest of the house. "This is how we do it!" … Robert's singing so loud to his favorite song by Montell Jordan. As I reach the very last step, Grandma yells, "come on here and eat, breakfast is ready ya'll"

We all sit together on Sunday mornings; it's the closest we'll ever get to actually doing something as a family since Robert hates going to church and Grandma allows him to make his own decision now that he's eighteen. She doesn't like it but she gets tired of going back and forth with Robert explaining to him the importance of going to church as a family. He just doesn't like church at all. I don't deem Robert to be an atheist or anything; maybe he's just going through a phase. I always did admire his ability to think for himself. No one can ever convince my older brother of anything. He was always the type to come up with his own philosophies and theories. Before seating myself with the rest of the family, I like to sit on the stoop to think about what I'll be wearing to church. Even though it's cold out, I'm used to the weather. I still enjoy the sunrays that beam right onto our house every morning. One thing about going to church I do enjoy is the fashion; what you wear always gets noticed.

While walking into church, I can feel the piercing of everyone's eyes, but that does not make me uncomfortable at all. I love the attention. Of course they're looking. I'm wearing pointed toe pink pumps, my brand new tight fitting knee length skirt, and pretty in pink blouse. My hair always falls perfectly. I am known for that. We sat down in our usual seats and my granny dove right into praise and worship, "Glory, glory father, thank ya," she wasted no time. Me, on the other hand, I treasured my personal relationship with God but I have never been into catching the "*holy-spirit*" and getting the crowd excited.

"Hallelujah!" Grandma fell to the floor. "Boom"! Here she goes again, I step out of the way, knowing the deacons and ushers were headed in our direction. I exit to the ladies room with my head throbbing. All of this noise is killing me.

"All crap," I think to myself. Out of all people why did I run into this lady? Sister Williams is so dramatic.

"Hello Sister Williams." I said nervously.

"Hey baby, is everything alright?" She responded suspiciously.

"Yes, I'm just fine."

Aaliyah quickly interrupts, "April what is going on with you?" Aaliyah always paid close attention to me. She could sniff out all clues to my mischief in a heartbeat.

"Aaliyah go away! I'm fine, just a little light head ache and I feel like I need to just sit down away from everything. Why aren't you in church anyway? Get back in there! Grandma is going to start looking for you and she'll come in here." I demanded grudgingly.

"Whatever it is April, you need to come clean, I know you're up to something young lady and when Granny finds out, she is going to beat you down." Aaliyah whispers with this odd but hysterical look on her face. She watches way too much "Law and Order" I think to myself as she leaves the bathroom.

Although I knew Aaliyah would find out things, I would never be the one to actually share them with her. I immediately run into the toilet stall, lean over and it feels like I am going to *die*. The pain in my stomach is unbearable. "Why is this happening to me?" Is my thought as I barfed; the smell itself would make any person sick. Still not feeling all the way together, I rush to the sink to rinse, pull my hair into a pony tail and get out of there before anyone else saw me like that.

By the time I got back, Granny and the kids were headed my way. "Chile come on here now, what in the world were you up to in that bathroom?" She fusses.

"Yeah April, what were you up to in there?" I cover Aaliyah's mouth immediately.

This girl just doesn't know when she has gone too far, little brat. "Nothing Gram, I just had a stomach ache, maybe it was the breakfast. I explained. And why are we leaving so soon?"

"I just remembered your Uncle Mike needed me to stop by today." said Grandma.

I was thinking to myself on the way home, tracing symptoms, and wondering what it could be that had me feeling so ill. As soon as we got home I rushed into the house and straight into our bedroom, picked up my journal and begin writing.

**Dear Journal**

*"I am feeling sick today and there is absolutely no one to talk to. My grandmother is so clueless most of the time, if I ever actually told her what I was really feeling she wouldn't be able to handle it at all. It's awful. Why would God do this to me? I'm stuck here in this hellhole with no one. I miss my mom like crazy even though she is a deadbeat. I can just imagine us being like sisters, dressing up alike, doing each other's hair and talking about everything. She just couldn't handle her life with us and left us with my old grandma who*

*is trying her best to raise us. Anyway, I have been meaning to write that I shared intimacy for the first time ever about two weeks ago. Donnie came over here to stay with me while Gram went to visit my uncle, her son Mike. Mike is sick with cancer but he's all Grandma has left since my mother couldn't bear the existence of herself. She's been gone for a while now. Anyway, I haven't had the chance to write since the day Donnie came over but he is the most amazing boy ever. I think what I love the most about him is his confidence. He just has this way about him that makes me fall in love over and over again. People say us young people know nothing about love. And I guess they could be right, especially since I have no one to have ever experienced love with; unless you count my annoying little cousins and big brother Robert. That is love but Donnie was much different. He listened to me and cared for me like a real "man". And the intimacy, it was nothing like what Destiny told me, she was already "doing it". Destiny, my school buddy, told me her first time was painful and scary. I on the other hand, with Donnie, the blood rushed from my head into the tips of my toes. I think I went into dreamland, la-la land or something. I heard nothing else but Donnie when he softly pulled my hair back and murmured the three magic words, "I love you." I was in paradise. I had never been loved by any man other than my big brother. Donnie was everything.*

"Boom, boom, boom!" "Open the door April, what the hell are you doing in the room? I need to get in there!" Robert screamed. Gasping for air I propped up. "You scared me. Okay Robert, hold on a minute." I scurried away my journal my secret untouched place so that I could be sure no one would ever find it.

"Girl, get the heck out of this room like somethin' is wrong with you or somethin'." Robert screamed.

"I have a head ache and I was trying to rest for your matter of fact."

"Well it makes no sense for you to lock doors as if you pay some bills around here lil girl." He says.

"Robert, please spare me with the unremitting reminder that you're the *'man'* around here okay."

"Un-un-re-un… what?" Robert stuttered. Where do you find all these big words?"

We both laughed and left the room.

I go into the kitchen where my grandmother spent most of her time and ask her if she needs help with anything. The lady hardly asked us to do anything around the house. Every now and then I felt it was my duty to assist her and get her off her feet. Gram was heaven sent to all four of us kids. I found myself often baffled at her children's current conditions and how they turned out to be so terrible; she was the sweetest thing I've ever known. Gram was the kind of woman who'd give away her last dollar to a stranger. And one time she even gave away her jacket to this woman on the street; took it right off her own back.

I cooked a light dinner; nothing like what my Grandma would have done but it served its purpose. I call everyone to the dinner table and again attempt the "family" thing. Robert comes to the table with his usual rants about religion and why we should all have our own beliefs and ways of thinking; as he speaks you can tell Gram is getting uncomfortable. My grandmother was a red bone, hazel-eyed beauty. Creole, is what she said she was, a mix of a few things, born and raised down in Louisiana. She turned very red in the face when she was upset and right now her face is on fire. Robert continued on with his blabber and suggested we all try different churches from different denominations. He felt strongly about his views and Aaliyah and Tyson were seriously listening to his every word. They were young but old enough to take in thoughtful expression. Gram told Robert to shut up and leave the table. "You have gone too far Robert. I need you to take your foolishness to another room. "Lord please forgive this boy, he doesn't know any better." My grandmother cried out. I just sat there and observed until it all simmered. By the end of the night all were asleep and in peace. The nights were usually that way. That's another difference between Gram and my mom. My mom hosted any and every one in her house. She didn't care what day, what time. If you were hungry or cold, you had a spot to crash at in my mother's house. All sorts of weirdo's came over. And I could definitely tell when she was gone because more and more crack heads would come stay with us. Yes, my mother would leave for days at a time. It went from a couple hours, a day, and then a few days, weeks and now … forever.

With those thoughts, I hop in the king size bed with Tyson and Aaliyah. Robert began sleeping on the floor once he turned about thirteen. He respected himself and us enough to do that. Robert was actually a gentleman although my grandmother didn't understand him. He took his brother/daddy role extremely seriously.

**

Another Cold day at John Mere High School, the bell rings and kids start fleeing like wild animals. Destiny comes running down the hall my way and I was hoping the stale look on my face would clearly indicate my lack of excitement for her shenanigans this morning, but I guess not.

"Oh my gosh, oh my gosh girl, did you hear the news about what happened over the weekend? Your best friend in the whole world was seen at the movies with Donnie. And what do you have to say about that?" She hurried and asked me. Donnie was the star running back at John Mere. He was every girls dream. Everyone has always known us as best friends and we should have kept it that way because the minute we made it official and public, everyone stuck their noses in our business.

Destiny didn't even give me a chance to digest the information. "What are you gonna do?" "Are you gonna dump him? That jerk!" Destiny didn't stop. The one thing I hated the most about Destiny was her instigating ways.

I cut the conversation with Destiny short, "I need to be on time for class so I really have to go." I clarified to her. " Just call me later on." I told her as I walked away.

 I got into class sat down and began thinking, I was better off just listening to the details Destiny had to spill because I spent that entire class period pondering over the fact that Donnie may have actually been seeing someone else. To make that situation more frustrating, it may very well be with a person who despises me the most. I knew Destiny was being sarcastic with that '*your best friend in the whole world*' line, because that person does not exist. I don't trust anyone enough to ever have a so-called best friend. What's more hurtful is Destiny knows I have no parents and no real connection to anyone the way I have connected with Donnie. She insists on hurting me. She seemed far too happy to share that gossip with me.

Meanwhile during math class, "Oh Miss Smith…" Mrs. Wilson sings, "Are you there? What is the square root of 55?"

"Um the square-root of 55 Mrs. Wilson is 7.4." I replied. Mrs. Wilson only called on me to check me back into reality. She knew so much about my life and history. She taught my brother Robert also. She sometimes played aid to my need for ears. I talked to her a lot but never about something that I would be too embarrassed for her to know. *"Ring!"*

Saved by the bell! I made sure I got out of that building without anyone seeing me. I hurry home, find my journal and plop right onto the couch

**Dear Journal,**

*I hate my life. Once, again! Just when I thought things were actually looking upright for me, I find out that I have been played once again. I had finally opened my heart and today it has been shattered. It's like every time I look up, someone is giving me solidification that I have no purpose here. To top things off, I'm still sick and I have not found out the reason for it. I just want to get away from here. I can't stop crying. I am shaking with despair and humiliation. The pain is sinking from my stomach into my back. I should be used to this sort of pain by now but I have never felt anything this horrific. Donnie is so stupid. I can't trust anyone at all.* "April come and get this phone chile," Grandma called. I snapped back into reality, it must be Destiny I thought to myself.

"One minute, I'm coming right out." I yelled back at Gram. I rushed to put my journal away and washed my face. I hurried to the kitchen and grabbed the phone as fast as I could.

"Destiny, what's up?"

"Well, April I thought you'd never ask. I was trying to tell you that Donnie was seen this weekend with Jessica."

"Which Jessica?" I questioned.

"The captain of the cheerleading team, Jessica! They say she was dressed real classy too; leather jacket with the new patterned leggings and her lipstick matching. She and Donnie went to the show to see 'Twilight'."

"Are you kidding me?" I shouted! I had been with Donnie last weekend also. Friday night I believe. Donnie would never do this! He told me that he loved me. I need to investigate this one. "I'll see you tomorrow Destiny." I hung up with that depressing feeling again. I knew it was a ruthless idea to believe Donnie was actually interested in me. I rush into the bedroom and drown myself in my pillow. Feeling nauseous, I scurry into the bathroom with my hand over my mouth. The door slams behind me and right away I hear three soft knocks on the door as I vomit a whole day worth of food into the toilet.

"It's me April!" in her small mouse voice. "Are you okay, can I get you anything?" Aaliyah was the sweetest yet devilish little girl in the world. I knew she just wanted information from me. Too bad I didn't have any, yet. I sat there on the bathroom floor in disgrace. Something just didn't feel right. I knew what I needed to do.

# Chapter 2

I can smell the mist of morning; I actually enjoy the winter cold. I sit outside for a moment as I'm conjuring up my next move. I need to be getting ready for school but here I am stuck in this mess. After a few minutes I realize that I am running a little behind my schedule; I hurry and get dressed and rush out the door walking and thinking about this Donnie and Jessica mess. I really thought he was genuinely into me but I should have listened to Destiny. When Donnie and I first thought about making things official, she was the very first person to tell me it was a terrible idea. She said that Donnie was the player type. I gave him the benefit of the doubt, but I should have kept to myself instead of giving him the power to hurt me.

Well, I finally catch up with Donnie and he approaches me with a kiss to the lips but I pull away.

"What in the world is wrong with you now?" Donnie asked.

"I heard about you and that ole girl you decided to go out with the other night. And you and I had seen each other that same night. What's the point Donnie?" I replied.

"Why do you always jump to conclusions? Jessica and I have been friends since grade school. When I had no one at all, she and her mother took great care of me growing up. They would make sure I had dinner and lunch, and sometimes they gave me rides to and from school. We just hung out as friends. Nothing more! What's the big deal?" Donnie explained.

"Why do you have to go to the one place everyone from John Mere High is going to be? It's embarrassing to have to get to school and hear all this crap. And if she's such a "friend" why didn't you invite me? Why did you two have to go solo, Donnie?" I cried with frustration.

"Well April, I don't have all the answers. I am not a perfect guy. I just didn't think it was a big deal. I'll make this up to you, I promise." Donnie kissed me on the forehead and ran into the building.

I was still upset but I guess he could be telling the truth. I mean everyone knows Donnie and I are seeing each other. I don't know who would pursue him anyway. At the end of the school day, I wait for Donnie at the front gate and here he comes running towards me with a ton of flowers. "Where on earth did you find these in this cold weather?" I asked Donnie.

"You must have forgotten. I'm only here half a day. I leave this place right at noon. So I went to the store and thought I'd put a smile back on your face."

I must admit it did make me happy to see that at the very least, he cared enough to try. And the students around us all saw how charming Donnie was with me. I hope this sets the record straight. And where was big mouth Destiny to see this? Destiny is always around to see the drama and never catches the good stuff. Regardless to what anyone says; Donnie makes me so happy. He held my hand and walked me straight home. I was on cloud nine. I totally forgot to tell him that I'd been feeling sick lately. I still need to figure out what was really going on. I scurried home and rushed into the bathroom and closed the door. I had Destiny bring me a pregnancy test to school earlier. She had a little more freedom than I did. Destiny got allowance every week and her parents allowed her to go into the store alone.

What is happening right now? Am I really sitting here about to pee on this stick? This is unbelievable.

I finally get enough balls to take the test. I sat the test on the sink, plopped down, and waited for my results. The phone rings and it's Destiny of course. I told her to call me at 4:30 and she was right on time. We had been on the phone all night last night talking about this possible pregnancy and weighed my options until we both fell asleep. "So what does it say?" She inquires.

"I'm too scared to look at it girl; I am going to faint right now." I pick up the test and there you have it, two pink lines. Right away I'm hearing three soft knocks on the door. Here she goes again! Aaliyah watched my every move. But I can't dare open the door. My life has ended. I immediately drop the phone and fall to my knees. My eyes are completely dry, can't shed a single tear, and the shock is completely overwhelming. My entire body is numb and I feel absolutely nothing. I rush into the bedroom and grab my backpack filling it with every piece of clothing possible. I have to get out of here. There is no way I can be here under this condition. My grandmother is going to kill me if she ever finds this out. This woman gave me a chance and I blew it. I blew it! But I need to talk to Donnie. So I calm myself down as much as possible. I was thinking about running. Running and never looking back. It didn't matter what I grabbed, I stuffed my bag, grabbed my journal, slammed my piggy bank into the floor and scrapped up any change I had. I ran out the door as fast as I could. As I am leaving Robert is right behind me rushing also. I asked him what his big rush was and he explains he is on his way to the hospital to check on his so-called girlfriend, Lauren. I pace back and forth and plopped to the ground. I sat there on the stoop pondering over whether or not I should call Donnie. I'm afraid he will not be happy with me at all. I've seen this situation play out far too many times in my life. Hell, my own father never wanted me, so I can only imagine what Donnie may have to say. I go back inside and grab my journal. I slowly drifted as I began writing.

**Dear Journal,**

*I wonder what it could be like to have a little family of my own. I never really dreamed of a family. I never really had one so I don't even know what that should look like but Donnie and I would make a perfect baby as far as looks go. I'd try my absolute best to be nothing like my dirty mother was. My mother was so cruel. It took me a long time to understand that the drugs had taken over her entire being. So I try not to have mean thoughts about her anymore. But my own mother would sell me for drugs. She'd let this big black guy, I never knew his name, come in and do whatever he wanted with me, in exchange for drugs. There was this one time, I'll never forget; he and this other guy, a little smaller than him, came into our bedroom and told the kids to get out. Robert wasn't there. My Uncle Mike use to take Robert everywhere with him, in hopes that he would be the one to take over when he got too sick to run the streets. Anyway, they came into the room and told me to take off all of my clothes. I did as they said because I already figured out the results of being insubordinate. I closed my eyes and prayed not to feel anything. I prayed so hard, I think I just blacked completely out. I had trained myself not to feel anything from that day forward. I taught myself not to feel. I hated my own mom growing up; I wonder how many kids can say the same?*

I snap out of it as Gram yells my name. "April … come get this phone!" I ran back into the house and Surprise, surprise, it's Donnie. "Hey baby," he says.

"Hi, Donnie, how are you? I've been meaning to call you; I really need to talk to you about something." I replied worriedly.

"What is it now? It's always something with you. Let's just catch up tomorrow." Donnie says.

"Okay Donnie."

I head into the room throw my bag onto the floor and finally fall asleep after tossing and turning, wrestling with my mind.

**

The sun is out this morning. Although it's still cold, I love the sun. It has a way of changing my entire mood. Rushing into the bathroom once every morning has become a part of my daily routine. I've gotten so good at keeping it as discreet as possible and lately Aaliyah hasn't been bothering me with her questions. As I'm getting dressed, I'm fighting with myself about what to wear and what colors I'll be bringing out today. My hair of course, is never a problem. Although lately I've been getting threats from crazy girls about cutting my hair off, probably Donnie's little chicks he flirts with, it's always something with him. I have never been able to keep many female friends because of my looks. If only they knew just how un-pretty I really felt all the time. It's like the saying, "walk a mile in my pumps, and you wouldn't last a minute."

"See ya'll later!" I announced to everyone as I rush out the door. Donnie meets me about half way with another dozen roses. I guess he wanted to cheer me up before I dropped another bomb on him. This time the flowers only let me know that he's probably done something wrong again and thought I had found out about it. Little does he know, that is the very last thing on my mind at this point. "Thanks for the beautiful roses, but what I wanted to tell you is that I took a pregnancy test because I had been feeling sick every morning and the test came out positive." Donnie's mouth fell to the floor. He was in total shock and disbelief. "Are you sure?" he says.

"I'm so sure." I reply. Donnie picks up his mouth and tells me he will have to see me later and that he needed to go do something. He rushes off. I didn't get another word out. At this point, I am completely lost. I really don't feel like going to school like this. I'll just continue down the street. I realize that I'm passing the school but oh well, there is no way I'm going in there to deal with all of this.

My neighborhood feels so different right now. I am in complete disarray I could be lost but at this point I really don't care. The disgrace filled my gut as I walked the street with my head hanging. After a few hours, I finally made it to a train station and decided I was headed south. Listening to all the noise around me on the train has ironically enough, given me a sense of peace within myself and I am able to take a nap. I was exhausted and overwhelmed. It was the best thirty minutes of my life. My nap would have continued if this idiotic man desperate for my attention had not interrupted it. The man kept nudging my knee, "Aye girl, aye girl." He said.

"WHAT!" I yelled back.

"Ma'am, I was only trying to tell you that this train ride is ending. You're going to have to reroute beautiful." He insisted.

"Oh my, I am terribly sorry for that. I have been through so much recently and I am being so rude. Forgive me would you?" I asked.

"Of course, anything for those beautiful brown eyes of yours, can I help you with anything?"

"Well, where exactly are you headed? Are you from out here?" I asked.

"Yes, I'm headed home actually. You want some food or something?"

"Um, well, I guess food has never hurt anyone. What is your name if you don't mind me asking?"

"My name is Bruce; Bruce Jackson to be exact."

"Well, Bruce Jackson, it's a pleasure meeting you. My name is April Smith. What time is it?"

"It is now, 11 o'clock and the pleasure is all mine, now let's go eat!" Bruce responded with enthusiasm.

I have no idea what town this is but it's kind of cozy. I immediately find a pay phone booth and express to Bruce that I need to make a phone call. With a concerned look on his face, "why, who are you calling?" It was weird that he'd have so many questions already. "I'm just calling my friend so at least one person will know where I am. Give me a second." The phone rings and after a few moments Destiny answers, "Hello …"

"Hey girl it's me, April."

"Girl, you had me worried when you didn't show up to 1st period. You know we have all these projects due because it's the end of the semester, where the heck are you?" Destiny inquired. "I'm in some hick town with this guy Bruce Jackson. I just needed to get away Destiny. I told Donnie this morning about the baby and he just left me standing there. I think I'm going to lose it if I don't figure out how to get rid of this baby soon." I responded.

"Well keep me posted with everything April. But you are really trippin' and you really should come home and let us figure out this stuff. The least you could do is make sure you finish H.S. this is our last year April. Get yourself together." Destiny went in on me. At least I could trust her to tell the truth if nothing else. "Alright girl, I will be calling you back soon."

I step out of the booth and I'm thinking to myself that this place reminds me of the old movies Robert and I used to watch as kids. For some reason I didn't feel the need to ask many questions, I just followed Bruce's lead. As we walked, Bruce asked me questions about my family and was curious about why I was even riding on that train all morning in the first place. Since he insisted, I gave Bruce the "4-1-1"! I'm

not sure he was ready for all I had to share but I figured I'd

rather get it over with sooner than later. I talked and he

listened. And I could feel his empathy right away. His eyes

began to water and he grabbed my waist and pulled me close.

I took a deep breath and laid my head on his chest. Bruce was

a gorgeous man; 6'3, dark brown skin with a nice clean cut.

For the first time in my life, I felt a sense of security.

Thirty minutes passed and we finally reached our destination.

Bruce opens the door and tells me to go on in. The restaurant

is old, but beautiful and has so much character. The people

inside stared as if they had never seen a black woman before.

And now I'm actually getting a little nervous.

"Let's sit down right here ma'am. And don't worry about the

stares; it's just that you're the most beautiful woman in town

right now. These folks ain't never seen nothing like it." He whispered. I giggled behind him as he continued to say things to me I'd never heard from a man before. He told me to get used to it because my beauty captivated him. He also made it clear that everything he has gotten to know about me has only made me even more beautiful. I tried hiding my smiles and began eating. I ate like it was my first meal in years. The breakfast was great; reminded me of my Granny's pancakes and eggs. I pulled my journal out and asked Bruce to excuse me for a moment.

### *Dear Journal,*

*I am pregnant! I may as well spit that out right away. And I am disgusted at myself for not being more responsible. I had given myself away to an idiot just ONE time and here I am. I am in this crazy small hick town with some stranger. Although he's a beautiful stranger, I don't know what I'm thinking. Maybe just maybe if I actually had some parents or even just one parent, I'd make better choices. I'm a stupid fool! But on a better note, it's nice to have Bruce, my stranger friend I just met. He's listens to everything I have to share and I can tell he's very much into me. I don't think I've ever had anyone listen this closely. He is so kind and sweet spirited. He's damn near perfect! At least that's how it feels right now. But the way my life works, no one is ever what he or she seems to be. I know he'll disappoint me with some lies or some crazy truth that'll come out soon. He could be some serial killer for all I know. But what in the world will he say when he finds out I'm pregnant? I really need to find out how to get an abortion and fast! I can't have a BABY right now. Maybe I should just tell him and let him help me figure this out. But what if it turns him away? I'm so lost right now. To top things off, I still have to deal with the fact that once 3 o'clock hits; my grandmother will definitely be looking for me. I'm literally a 'Runaway' right now.*

I stuff my journal back into my duffle bag and thank Bruce for allowing me that time. "Thanks, I get in these moods where I really can't focus until I free my thoughts. It's just my way of calming down I guess. Why are you so patient? I've never seen anyone like it before?" I ask.

Bruce laughs and responds, "Your beauty is my virtue right now. I'll be the most patient person in the world if it means I can be in your presence."

I laugh out loud. "Boy you sound like some ole sugar daddy or something."

He quickly shuts me down and almost scares me a bit, "Sugar Daddy! Never! I'd never make myself out to be some womanizer like that. I hate men who take advantage of women. I can't stand that. Don't ever make a mistake by saying something like that ever again!"

For the first time, Bruce showed me a little angry side of him. I began thinking to myself; there is more to this guy than what I've been seeing for the last few hours. For now, I'll calm him down and apologize. But I see I better be careful with my words with him. We gather our food and he tips the waitress.

As we left the beautiful diner, He wrote his number on a small sheet of paper and stuck it in my back pocket. We proceeded back to the train station. I waved to him and ended it with a sweet blow kiss. By the look on his face I could tell that I had left a strong impression on this guy and he had done the same to me. As great as I felt with Bruce, I was headed back to my misery. I really needed to get my life in order and fast.

**

I made it back home right on time. My head was spinning, but I hurried up and called Destiny. She gave me the logistics of the happenings at school and I told her everything about this perfect stranger Bruce. "Girl he was so fine. Tall and handsome, he even has dimples. He seemed like he was very intelligent and well mannered. You ain't gone find that in the hood." I described everything I could remember.

"Girl you sound sprung already. You just met this guy. And what about Donnie and this baby?" Destiny questioned. Destiny didn't allow us much time to fantasize. "Girl what are you waiting on?" She said.

"I know Destiny, I'm about to go ahead and start collecting these funds. As a matter of fact I need to get in contact with Robert. I haven't heard or seen him since yesterday." I explained. We both hung up at the same time right after a quick "talk to you later." I dialed Robert's number, but there was no answer. Tried again and still nothing so I decided to leave him a message on his answering machine explaining the seriousness of the call. Aaliyah pushes her way in the room right over the clothes piled up against the door. "What's up April? How was school today?" She asked.

"School was just fine, now go find you some business little girl." I quickly responded. My Grandma called me into the kitchen asking questions about school. "So April, if school was just fine why would Mrs. Wilson call me concerning your absence today and also shared with me that you've been really spaced out during her class lately?"

"Um ... I don't know why she would call you Grandma, but today I had a meeting with the student council and forgot to check in with Mrs. Wilson afterwards. I have been a little wondering lately because I already know the work we're doing in there. It's boring!" I was so convincing, Grandmother showed no concern at all after that drama I had given her. I learned early how to lie. My own momma did it every day back when I was younger. She'd come home for short period of times, promising us she'd return soon. I'd stare outside when the streetlights were off, praying for her return. While my big brother had given up hope long before I did, I cried myself to sleep most nights back then. Probably the most painful years of my life were the ones I had to face reality with my mother's drug addiction. I was about 10 years old. I started to put the pieces together when something embarrassing and tragic occurred. I will never forget the day …

*We walked into the dark house, lights cut off again. Robert and I had gotten so used to our lights being off, that wasn't the shocker as we entered. Robert stumbled over someone lying on our living room floor. Right away there was a loud scream for help coming from a room in the back of the house. "Somebody please call 9-1-1!" the scream got louder. Robert pushed me behind the couch, the only piece of furniture left in the room. "Don't move!" he demanded. He ran to the back and all I heard was a loud lump to the floor. I ran as fast as I could. At that time, it felt like it took me all of five seconds to wrap around to the back of the house. My brother was lying there shaking and crying. He was the first face I saw. But next* to him was a man bleeding. The red was flowing like the Mississippi river. I was sick to my stomach at that point but I knew I needed to do something. I ran into the bathroom in hopes of releasing this nauseous feeling into the toilet. And there she was, my mother was passed out holding a knife covered in blood. As awful she had been to me in my life, I knew I couldn't call the police. Not now. I wanted to save my mother from herself. And who was this man who I assumed was dead here on the floor? I had no idea. I grabbed the knife with a towel, wiped the handle, walked into the kitchen and placed it in the hands of the "dead man." Called 9-1-1 and told them a man got high in my house and killed himself. Once I made that call. I slapped my mother to wake her and told her to leave. Whether or not the police actually believed it is a whole other story. But they couldn't do much to prove anything. To be honest, I don't think they cared enough to even fully investigate the situation entirely. After that, my life *went into an uproar, as if it could have gotten any worse. I told my mother to go, to get out of there and she literally ran. This was the last time Robert and I had seen our mother.*

"April … what in the world is wrong with you girl. You been sitting here in la-la land for the last fifteen minutes?" Grandmother yelled. I snapped back and realized I was supposed to be figuring out this abortion stuff. "Sorry Grandma, you know how I am but anyway, have you heard from Robert?" I asked.

"No, I haven't heard, maybe you need to go see about your brother. I'm thinking he is with that little girlfriend of his. I remember him saying something about a car accident she was in.

# Chapter 3

*(Days Ago)*

*Robert ...*

Every time I call Laruen she is pressing the ignore button. I am sick and tired of this. The only woman I've ever loved outside of my lil sista' and grandma; is acting like we're strangers. This woman is pregnant with my baby. Well, at least that's what she told me but I am starting to believe this girl is up to no good. I just can't understand how a woman could ever deny a man who actually wants to be a part of their shorty's life. My father was never around. I couldn't tell you whether he preferred apples or oranges, red or blue. The only thing I know about the man is his name. I barely know his age; I speculate that answer based on the half-truths my mother used to tell when she got drunk every night. When they met and how old they were when they did this and that. My mom was crazy stuck on that man. I really think she became an addict because of him yet I've tried to ignore that idea just in case I ever get to spend some time with Frank and make my own judgment.

"Gram, I'm stepping out aight?"

Okay suga, you be safe out there, come home in one piece." Grandma asserted.

"I got you ma!" I promised my Grandmother one thing and one thing only, that she would never have to come looking for me and find me laid up dead somewhere. With the way the news reported every night, there was a least one dead black man with a sheet over his body. That was one of my Grandma's greatest fears.

A typical Philly, January night, I was freezing my ass off in my old 'L-dog'. I love my Cadillac but the heat wasn't kicking the way it did when I first bought it. The cheap

dealers on Western suited up those cars just to get them off

the lot. There ain't no telling what the hell was wrong with lil

ole Betsy. But she gets me from point A to point B, that's all

that matters at this point. I'm driving down Madison to holla'

at my boys; I can always catch them out there tryna keep

some food on the table.  Most of us did. It was the only thing

that got passed down to us from our daddy's and uncle's and

them. It was as if we had no other choice. How does a young

"nigga" avoid the streets? The streets are all we got. We feel

powerful out here like we own some shit. The only place a

black man can walk around with his chest poked out and head

high. Street cred is like being the CEO's son. You walk

around untouchable and the whole world kisses ya ass all day.

Of course until daddy is fired or (for us) your credibility

becomes questionable. Which a lot of people been out here

snitching lately so it's been a lil bare. Once that happens, you're out there on your own like everybody else. But until then, you live on top of your world. I finally catch up with T.J.

"What's up fam, everything alright out here?" I ask him.

"Everything is everything, another day, another dolla'. You know how it is out here man. I'm just tryna stay out of trouble." T.J. explains.

"I already know. I need a favor from you though. I got this chick I been dealing with and she's pregnant but I'm not sure if it's mine because since she's been pregnant, she's been keeping her distance and fell back. I don't know what the hell is going on. I need to find this chick and get some answers bro."

"What, get the hell outta here man. Yeah, I'm down just tell me when and where. I got you." T.J. assured. I always knew I could count on T.J. He has always been there for me since way back and we've never fallen out.

We both hear sirens and of course that means it's time to bail out. I immediately get out of the way and head to Lauren's house to see if I could catch her before I send the goons out.

***

"Beep, beep, beep" is the sound I'm hearing as I watch her suffer on the hospital bed. I scream, "Can someone please come and help her?" I was praying to myself, "God, if you'll listen, I know I haven't been going to church and I have done some very bad things, but please don't take her life. I haven't gotten the chance to meet my precious son or daughter yet. This baby is going to need a mother." "CAN SOMEONE PLEASE COME AND HELP US?" I yelled at the top of my lungs this time. Lauren looks as if she is going to take her very last breath. What a shit hole of a hospital, these people don't care whether you live or die. To get that call this evening that Lauren had just been in an accident as I was on my way to see her wasn't a coincidence. She needed me and I was only a couple minutes away.

The doctors rush in after what felt like a lifetime and asked me to step out of the room because they were about to take her into the operation room for emergency surgery. He also expressed that there was a chance to save the baby, but by the looks of things, Lauren may not make it. I trembled with fear. I couldn't sit down, my heart was beating through my chest and I felt numb. I was wondering who would be a good person to call in a time like this but couldn't think of anyone whom I thought cared enough to tell me what I needed to hear in this moment. I always portrayed myself as tough but the truth is I have never been in love with a person like this ever before. In my mind, I thought I was going to marry this girl someday. I was only waiting for the right time to really make things official.

Lauren's family enters and her mother is hysterical. Mrs. Carter was as sweet as pie, cared for me like a son of hers.

Her father on the other hand, he was always the 'jerk'. He was a corporate executive and I don't think he ever took his corporate hat off.

"What happened to my baby, Robert? Please tell me Lauren is okay." Mrs. Carter said as she cried on my shoulders.

"I'm really not sure mamma. I got a phone call from a friend and rushed straight here. So far, Lauren's condition is not good." I explained.

"Where is God in all of this? Why would He do this to me, I've done everything right? I just don't understand. And I told her to stay home and stop being outside so much with my grandbaby on its way." Mrs. Carter cried like a baby. I held it together for her sake. But I could most definitely relate to what she was feeling.

I must admit I was slightly intimidated by Mr. Carter's presence so I kept quiet for the most part. I let the family take care of the business and tracking of Lauren's status as I sat there trying my best to be patient. When suddenly, in walks this tall light-skinned man with dreads on his head.

"Travis, hey how are you? We have been asking about you and your schooling." Mr. Carter greeted.

"I've been just fine but where is my girl Lauren, and my baby boy? How are they doing? I went about ninety miles per hour getting here." Travis responded.

Mr. Carter then explained to Travis. "They're in the operating room; we have yet to find out much of what's happening. We are just praying for a miracle right now."

Baby… baby boy? I let that soak in for a minute before approaching the situation. "Who the hell is this dude?" I think to myself. I knew something was fishy about Lauren's recent behavior but I was not trying to believe she would ever play me like that. Of course the idea that this baby could possibly not belong to me has been at the forefront of my mind since

Laruen didn't want me to touch her or even see her since the pregnancy. But the fact that Mr. Carter knows this man and accepts him has my blood rushing and I think I'm about to snap. "What you mean your baby?" I approach Travis.

"You must be Robert. Hi Robert, now is not the time to discuss all of this. Let's focus on Lauren's health right now and talk about everything else later." Travis said in a fearful tone.

"Naw, ain't no later bruh. We're going to talk about this shit right now. I have no time to sit here and waste. Now, what's up with you and Lauren?"

"Well Robert, you obviously don't know me, but I do know quite a bit about you. I think it is best you just relax and take your seat."

"Don't insult my intelligence dude, I ain't no dummy and I will literally break ya neck." I threaten Travis.

Mr. and Mrs. Carter had been asked to go into the operating waiting area to discuss some things privately. Therefore, nothing was holding me back. I raised my right hand and balled my fist headed for his nose. "POW!" Before I know it, I'm hit and blacked out immediately.

"Uh… sir, are you okay?" I here this very soft, sweet voice ask." My eyes slowly open and it feels like I just hit a brick.

"Hi, yeah I'm okay. I'll be fine." I replied.

"I have been trying to wake you for the past ten minutes do you need anything, water maybe?"

"Sure I'll take some water." I was devastated and embarrassed yet took her up on that water offer before I passed out again.

Mr. and Mrs. Carter came back into the waiting area inquiring about what happened between Travis and me. I immediately cut them off and ask about Lauren, "Forget about all that, what is going on with Lauren?" With a regretful look on her face, Mrs. Carter explained, "Well, she has gone through surgery and seems to be coming back to us. She is in recovery right now. Just keep praying. But the baby, the baby did not survive the accident." Mrs. Carter cried hysterically after those words. She leaned over as if the world's strongest man had punched her in the stomach. I even had to catch her from falling. Am I wrong for secretly being a little bit thrilled; not at the death of an unborn baby but Lauren was all over the place since the start of that pregnancy. Somewhere inside I was hoping to get the old Lauren back. We were really just friends, been friends for a very long time but after all of this, I've realized that I really do have feelings for her and that maybe I need to let Lauren know as soon as possible, how I really feel about her.

Travis finally returns with a cocky look on his face. I could just kill this 'nigga'! But I kept my cool (for now) and let him and Mrs. Carter talk. I was trying to be sensitive to his loss. I guess it was his loss. Who knows! I'm just praying for my girl. "Lord, or whoever you are, if you're there, please bring my soul mate back to me. I can't live; I don't want to live without her." My phone is blowing up. Gram keeps calling me so I finally call her back.

"Is everything okay with you boy?" Grandma asked.

"Yes, Ma everything is fine. I've been here at the hospital. Lauren got into an accident and lost the baby tonight. But they say Lauren is in recovery so do what you've done ma, you know… pray. I'm sure God will listen to your prayers before he'll hear mine" Granny was astonished when I told her to pray. She stumbled over her words, "Oh, oh, okay. I will do just that. And son, life has its way of kicking us until we get it straight. Keep on living. It's gonna be alright." I hang up with Gram and give Mr. and Mrs. Carter my goodbye's letting them know I'll be back bright and early tomorrow morning.

Riding through the city always gave me a sense of peace. The lights, the blistering breeze coming through my cracked window, somehow helped soothe me and I felt at ease. Lauren and I have been best friends since I can remember. I used to take my sister to Lauren's house sometimes when mom would be on her one of her binges. We both actually spent a lot of time with Lauren and her family. She comforted me and was always willing to listen whenever I needed her to and she has never shared any of those things.

**

After crashing at a friend's house I woke up to a voicemail from my baby sis. I called April back and asked what the emergency was that she needed help with. She answered, "Robert, I really need your help but I don't know how to tell you this. It's best I just spit it out. I'm pregnant and I need money for an abortion. Oh, and I need you to take me." She confessed.

"What the hell April, you have gone way too far now!" I yelled.

"I … I just really need you to help me right now and not judge me. I made a mistake, one time. Please Robert." April pleaded.

"I would ask you who, what, when but then I'm going to want to kill somebody." I was furious with April but I knew I was all she had. It's always been this way. I picked April up out of any ditch she ever dug for herself. This of course beats any other hole she has ever been in but I saved money for instances like this. There is no damn way this girl will be having any babies anytime soon. So this is fa sho an emergency. April is in no way shape or form ready to be taking care of another human being. She still needs to finish high school and I have hopes of her at least attempting the college thing. April has the brains to become anything she puts her mind to. I just pray she is nothing like our mother. With those thoughts, I hurried and called one of my home girls to find out which facility to take April to and immediately set an appointment. I know everyone else has given up on us. But I refuse to leave April hanging.

# Chapter 4

*April …*

My brother finally calls me back and I am able to spill the beans. He was upset, but his reaction wasn't as bad as I thought. Robert is a very patient person; it takes a lot to upset him but I guess he figured, who else was going to help a poor little girl like myself. Whatever the case, I am just glad to finally get this over with. I grab the phone to call Destiny.

"Hey girl, I finally got a hold of Robert, he is going to take me later on today to get this abortion." I explained.

"Oh wow, that is so good. I know you are so relieved." Destiny replied.

"Yeah, I'm happy but it's still sort of scary knowing what I am getting ready to do. This is a life. A whole life I am responsible for. It has a beat Destiny. This is tragic. On the flip side; the more I think about the kind of mother I had, the more I assure myself that I am making the best decision. Besides, how much of a mother can I be if I don't even graduate high school? I'll never be a deadbeat mom." Destiny and I talked for hours. She shared her opinion on abortion and told me about a time her older sister went to get one and how she slept for days afterwards. I became more nervous than I was before hearing about Destiny's sister. Yet, I was glad to at least have Destiny to talk to because if not for her I would be going insane trying to get through all of this on my own.

After hanging up with Destiny I decided to give Donnie a call to at least let him know what I was getting ready to do. I'm sure he'd be happy about the choice anyway.

The phone rings three times and Donnie finally answers in his deep raspy voice, "Hey youngin', how are you?" He says.

"I'm okay. Wondering why I haven't heard from you yet? You just ran off and didn't even bother to call me. But I'm over it; I just wanted you to know that I'm getting an abortion today." I said to him.

"WHAT! Why would you go and do that? I hadn't called you yet because I was just getting some things together for us. I just knew I needed to get the job done. I have been out hustlin' trying to make ends meet. You can't tell me something like that and just expect me to do nothing." He stated with aggression.

Donnie was serious about this, I thought to myself.

"Wow Donnie, the way you just left me hanging, I just put all thoughts about this baby to the side and I figured it would be best for the both of us if we discontinued the pregnancy. My life is already draining as it is."

"What is so draining about your life April? You are just like the rest of us. No one is living in some perfect fairytale." Donnie stated.

"Only if you knew the half D. Just know that I am making the best decision for us both."

"If you say so." He replied.

We both hung up at the same time. Even though neither of us said goodbye, I guess we both knew there was nothing left to say.

### *Dear Journal,*

*I am wrestling with myself about making this decision. I don't want to disappoint Donnie. And I actually believe he'll make a great dad to someone one day. He just has no idea the turmoil I've been through when it comes to "so-called" family. The idea of family sounds good but not in my world. I'll probably never know what that's like.*

*I remember when I first started my menstrual cycle at about nine years old and being confused about why my mother was so upset. She was really pissed and said so many curses of my name. She even kicked me in the stomach. I just remember crying in my pillow asking God why? I became very spiritual at a young age. I guess I was forced to understand that there must have been something more powerful than myself and all the pain I was experiencing. Had there not been; I would not have made it. I asked God over and over again, "Why me, what did I do to my mom for her to hate me so much?" I cried myself to sleep that night and first thing in the morning, my mom brought me some pills and forced me to take them every day from that day forward. Later to find out that she had me*

*on birth control.*

After about fifteen minutes, Robert came through the front door and rushed me to put on my clothes so that we could get going. I did exactly that. My Grandmother and Aaliyah were of course all in our business asking us where we were going. "What's the big rush?" Grandma asked. Luckily, Robert did all of the talking. "We're just going to see Lauren before she goes into surgery." Robert lied. Not sure why he chose that lie in particular but whatever the case it got Grandma off my back.

**

I get into Robert's old caddy, lean my seat back and let the music tune out my reality. My head has been spinning for the last couple of hours. I glare out the window and Robert tunes me completely out. I was waiting for him to say something but he never budged. "I guess he wasn't lying when he said he wasn't going to ask me anything. I just didn't believe it. Once we made it to the clinic; I took my first step out of the car and nearly collapsed. The feeling was as if a knife interrupted my intestines and hit my spine. The pain was unbearable, and knowing I was making a very permanent decision really spoke to me. My grandmother raised me as a Christian and I was taught that God knows our name before we even get to the womb. He knows exactly who we are and made us all perfectly in His image. So who am I to make a life or death decision for someone that God already knows? I don't think I can go through with this. This thought resonates as Robert takes my arm and practically drags me in. This place is cold and very quiet. You could hear a pin drop. This only added to my anxiety as I stood in line to sign in. I added my name to the list and gave them my medical card. The palm of my hands were so wet, the receptionist asked,

"Sweetie, are you okay? Would you like a cup of water or a towel?"

"No thank you, I'll be fine" I responded. I quickly found a seat because I was starting to feel weak in the legs again. I could literally hear the sound of the clock. As I scanned the place, it was colorless with pale yellow paint on the walls and no decorations at all. The girl next to me looked like she was about 13 or 14 years old. Sitting with her mother, she had silent tears rolling down her flushed cheeks. Her mother had what seemed to be a permanent frown on her face; she was obviously disgusted. This didn't help me at all. This place was creepy. Every hour they called about five names at once.

"Ashley Jones, Tish Roberts, Stephanie Coleman, Jammie T. Green, and Savannah Williams; come on in." The medical assistant said. They looked terrified. A couple of them looked as though they had lost color in the face, just pale.

"I really can't do this." I begin thinking to myself. Every "what if" came across my mind as I was forced to sit there and sulk in my misery for hours. All I could think about was how... how did I get here?

# Chapter 5

"April Smith, Tiffany Carter, Gracey Jones, and Kate Britton please follow me into your rooms." The assistant called. My heart fell to my knees. Robert looked at me and I could tell he felt my nervousness. He touched my shoulder and promised me everything would be okay. "I'll be right here the entire time." He said. I finally stretched out of my chair and proceeded into the hallway. My room was at the very end. She told me to take off all my clothes and put on the gown as she left the room. At this point, my heart rate is definitely abnormal, my stomach is starting to cramp and my back is giving out on me. This is the most painful experience and I haven't even started with the procedure.

"Alright April, we are going to check your height and weight first, then your vitals to make sure everything is normal and ready for surgery." The nurse says.

"WHAT surgery?" I yelled. "I thought this was more like a procedure, much more simple than a surgery. I didn't think I was getting a surgery done today."

"Okay ma'am. Remain calm and let's talk a little before we continue. First, it is a surgery. It is not a major surgery, but that is still the proper terminology for what you will be getting done today. We will be putting you to sleep for about forty-five minutes and we will be going inside and terminating the pregnancy." She explained. "Now, are you fully aware of what it is that we are doing today?"

I took a deep breath as I replied, "Yes, I am now aware and ready." My eyes filled with tears and I couldn't control them from rolling down my face.

"Miss Smith, are you going to be okay? This is difficult for anyone, but I've seen it a zillion times and it's not going to harm you in anyway. You will have to rest for about a week and you may experience a little heavy bleeding, but other than that you will be fine." The nurse assured me.

I know I am making the best decision but it isn't easy. I am not sure I'll ever forgive myself for this. I finally told the nurse that I was okay and ready to proceed. "Let's get it over with." I demanded.

I was taken into another room where there were two other girls waiting for their surgery. The anesthesiologist walked over to me and placed a mask over my mouth and nose. I immediately fell into a deep slumber.

The nurse taps my shoulder. "We are all done here sweetie. It's time to head to the recovery room."

"Recovery room?" I asked.

"Yes, it's just a place where you can relax for a while just to make sure everything is one hundred percent before you leave us; we make sure you are not bleeding too much and are not having any severe cramps. We will only keep you for another hour." She insisted.

"Okay then. I guess I have to sit still then." I cried.

I cried because I knew I had to face these other girls and I just felt more shameful. I was completely embarrassed but today I guess if nothing else, I discovered that I do have some self worth. I guess I saw myself in a much better light than this. I knew I was better. I knew I deserved better. As crazy as it sounds, after all I've been through, I still held myself to much higher standards. Most people look at the women that come into a clinic like this and figure they deserve to be here. They pass judgments and assume that we just belong in a clinic. I was once one of those people. Now look, after one short time with Donnie, I am the one that's here. I'll never let this shit happen ever again. There was this girl in the recovery room telling her story about her boyfriend leaving her in some parking lot after she told him she was pregnant.

"The nigga just left me there looking stupid. We had got into a fight earlier that day because I found out he was sleeping around with some cluck and I just couldn't understand why he'd cheat on me with that trash. These guys will lay down with anything and it's disgusting." She continued. The girl kept us entertained the whole hour.

As I walked back into the waiting area I saw Robert sitting in the exact same seat he was in when I left earlier.

This gave me so much comfort. I love my brother for always being here for me. Robert is the only person that has shown me consistency. He grabbed my hand and helped me walk outside and into his car. We were silent the whole ride home.

The first thing I did when I got home was hug my grandma for about a long two minutes and then picked up the phone to call Donnie.

"Hello." He answered.

"Hey Donnie. I made it back home. It's done." I told him.

"Wow, I still can't believe it's all over just like that. I mean, I really thought about becoming a dad. I was actually getting myself mentally prepared." He explained.

"Well, that's good you were willing to take on that responsibility, but save it for when you're one hundred and ten percent ready." I told him.

"Honestly April, that was real selfish of you to go ahead with that shit. I'm actually pretty fucked up over it. Don't even want to talk about it no more." Donnie said.

"Well Donnie. You have the right to feel how ever you feel."

"Yeah, and I think we need some space." Donnie stated.

"Wow Donnie, really? After all this, if nothing else, we had a friendship." I cried. He didn't respond. That was it. That was the end of the conversation. I just hung up the phone.

There wasn't exactly much I could argue with Donnie. I just left it alone. I crawled into my bed and cried myself to sleep.

**

As I am waking up I begin feeling those cramps everyone mentioned to me beforehand. I feel like shit. I gather myself together and grab the pain medication and a glass of orange juice hoping no one else wakes up behind me. This is something I recalled on one of those sitcoms. Never in a million years did I actually think I'd be that girl. My pain was at ease after about an hour and I was able to get back into the kitchen to make breakfast for everyone. I liked to show my grandma appreciation by keeping her off her feet from time to time. It felt great to sit with my family after all that I had endured the past few days. To make things even better, I could eat and smell my favorite foods without feeling nauseated. After breakfast I remember I hadn't spoken to Destiny in a while. I picked up the phone to give her the 4-1-1.

"Hey Destiny, it's been a while since I've seen you. What's the latest? Anything new going on?"

"Nothing new girl. It's only been a couple days. This has literally been the driest time of the year. The winter seems like its never going to end and all of us just seem like we're just trying to get through the school year." Destiny replies.

"True. We are girl. At this point that's all that matters. I've been kind of thinking about calling that strange nice looking guy I met on the train that day. I just remembered that he wrote his number down for me."

"What girl?" She hollered.

"Yes, after all the confusion between Donnie and I; I realized things would never be the same. I really think I'm ready for something new. Donnie literally hates me for getting this abortion and I have no energy to waste trying to get him to understand. He actually thought we were going to be this little family." I replied. Destiny and I both laughed out loud after I said that.

"Donnie just seems so much smarter than that. Why would he want a baby right now? The dude is really trippin'. But yeah girl, find his number and call him then if that's what you want to do. Just don't get too caught up girl. You don't even know the guy. He could be some crazed serial killer or something."

"Girl what!" I laughed to her.

"I'm laughing, but I'm still serious. Just be careful."

"I understand. I am. You act like I said I'm going to marry the guy or something. I just said I was thinking about calling him." I fussed back at Destiny for at least another hour. "Girl I am going to call you back. I need to catch up with Donnie one more time before I do anything else." I said.

"Okay then April, let me know what happens." She replied.

Donnie answers the phone after a couple call attempts. "Hey Donnie" I said in the most somber tone I could dig up.

"What's up April? I really don't want to deal with the small talk right now let's just cut to the chase."

"Well we ended on a bad note last night so I'm really just trying to see where your head is." I replied back.

"I'm just shocked to find out that you are foolish just like you mother was and you have no decency about yourself."

"Wow who knew all these years of friendship would be thrown out of the window like this. You're rude and inconsiderate but I'm mature enough to accept that and move on. You have no idea how much trouble I just saved you." I told him.

"Aren't you some kind of Christian or something? Isn't that against the commandments? You didn't even allow us the time to try and figure things out. But whatever I am done. You go and live your life. Finish school and stuff since that's the most important thing in your life." Donnie said.

"Yes, I am not even going to respond to your ignorance. You take it easy Donnie." We both hung up immediately. I can't believe how Donnie is acting right now. He questioned my religion and is showing no support at all. Instead of taking it personally and getting depressed I decide to go ahead and contact Bruce. I dug in my bag right away and found that small piece of paper in the back pocket of the pants I wore that day. I dialed his number. The phone rings three times and he finally picks up.

"April I have been waiting for you to call me."

"Bruce, how did you know it was me calling?" I asked.

"Well I gave you my personal number and I don't know anyone else that would call me from that area code." Bruce replied.

"Oh, wow. Well I guess that's a good thing. I had been thinking about calling you for a few days now but I've been so busy with school and everything. What's new on your end?" I asked.

"School, what are you in school for?"

"I am in my first year of college. Studying psychology." I lied because I was not sure of Bruce's age but I knew for a fact he was older than I was and I didn't want him to become uninterested because of my age. I'll be eighteen soon anyway and it will not make much of a difference. Besides, I am meeting with the counselor to figure out how I can graduate early.

"Psychology, wow that's deep. You must have a lot of fun studying people's brains and behaviors. I would have gone that route had I not started producing films at such a young age." Bruce gave me the run down of his career and it was surreal. He explained that he's worked with a ton of celebrities and is even the man behind a couple of my favorite movies. "How can such a successful guy live in such a boring town? No offense, but there is absolutely nothing going on in that hick town."

"Oh you definitely offended me." Bruce laughed. "But you are right. The only reason I keep my house there is because I grew up there. But I spend a lot of my time in Los Angeles."

"Wow, I've never been to LA, but I've always wanted to go." Just when the chat with Bruce gets interesting in comes little nosey rosy. "Hey April, what are you in here doing? You were in bed all night last night. Why'd you go to bed so early April?" Aaliyah asks.

"I was getting my beauty rest. Now go away little girl." Aaliyah sure does know how to ruin something.

"Okay Bruce I am not going to hold you from your very busy life. Let me allow you to get your work done and I'll do the same." I told Bruce.

"Okay but I hope it doesn't take you another three to five days to call again. I don't think I can go that long without hearing your voice." He replies.

"You sure do know the right things to say Bruce." I giggled.

"I'm just telling the truth. So I hope that means you'll call me later tonight." He requested.

"Sure Bruce. I can do that."

I hung up the phone in awe of what had just happened. Wow Bruce is really something else. I thought to myself.

"Now, Aaliyah what is it you want with me?"

"I am bored, lets play UNO." Aaliyah pleads.

"Okay, I'll play one game with you before I take a nap. I need my rest."

Aaliyah and I played a few games of UNO until she crashed. She was actually the first between the two of us to fall asleep. But I closed my eyes right after her. All I hear is my grandmother's big voice coming from the other room.

"APRIL!" Grandma hollered. It startled me and I quickly rose from the bed and go see about her.

"I need you to straighten this house and start washing the dirty laundry. Fold everything and place it where it belongs. I was so annoyed by her request. Too bad I couldn't tell her how messed up I was feeling. FML (eff my life) this sucks.

# Chapter 6

*Robert …*

Driving west to pick up Bud from the block, I start thinking about how my sister really needs for me to stay on top of her. April really has me worried now. She never took well the fact that we don't have parents, but now I'm starting to think she out here lookin' for a daddy or something. She used to be much stronger than what I've been seeing from her lately. Getting pregnant and shit …I told her she was gunna have to get over all the crazy shit we've been through and really focus on herself, but she is obviously still searching for something. She let that lil' nigga punk her; I should go over there and let him know what I can do to him. My phone rings and interrupts my thoughts. It's Lauren.

"Robert, hey where have you been? I thought you would've come to see me by now." She says.

"Wassup yo, nah I couldn't make it. I've been dealing with my little sister. How are you feeling?" I asked.

"I'm okay, I've had better days but just taking things one day at a time like you said Robert. Just trying to get better and back home."

"Yeah you need to get out of that place. Hospitals are for suckas." I joked with her.

Laughing out loud she replies, "Yes you're right and I'm tryna be sucka-free like you."

"Since it's getting late I'll let you rest and get up there tomorrow." I told her.

"Okay Robert. See you tomorrow."

"I love you." I hesitated but I knew I meant it.

"I love you too Robert." Laruen responded right away.

Wow, I do. I love Lauren. I didn't even ask her about the Travis dude. I just want to start fresh and leave it alone. But I am a man before anything, let me run into that fool again and he'll find out really quickly what I'm about. Lauren has her trust issues with me because she's seen a lot of my past relationships. She and I have been friends for a while and never really crossed that friend boundary until recently. I make it to Bud's house and he was excited to see me as usual. "What's up big timer?" Bud yells.

"What's up with you fam? How you been? You've been good out here man?" I replied

"Yeah, it's all good here. Just tryna stay afloat."

"Aight man let's head back to the crib. I need to check on my old lady."

Bud talked my ear off the entire ride about some business plan he had that he wanted me to help him with. Bud always came up with different "business" ideas. They weren't terrible, but his mind only went so far. He would always an idea, but no skill on how to actually execute it. Not to mention, most of the ideas required funds to start. Ever since my Uncle Mike has been sick, money has been tight. Mike wanted me to take over his territory but I just didn't feel like I was that kind of guy. Don't get me wrong, the money would be great but Mike was no one to trust and I can't run up behind someone I can't even trust myself. Ain't no tellin what dirt he's left behind for the next person to clean up. We made it to my grandma's house where Tyson and Aaliyah run to the front door at a very fast pace. "Robert" they both yelled.

"What have you two knuckle heads been up to?"

"We have just been wondering where you been?" Tyson replied.

"Yeah, I know. There has been a lot going on these days. Where is April?"

"She's been in that room all day long." Aaliyah responded. I immediately head into the back of the house to check on grandma and April. Grandma looked a little distraught. I picked up her feet and just rubbed them for a minute. "Hey, Robert. I've been praying for your friend and you. Been worried about you." Grandma says.

"I appreciate that but no need to worry about me. I will always be good."

"You know your Uncle Mike hasn't had any good reports lately. You should go out there and see about him. He's the last bit of family we have you know?"

"Word, what they sayin' now? I will go and check on him soon Ma."

"And check on that crazy sister of yours. The teacher called and said she has not been focused in class, and as a matter of fact, she had the nerve to miss a class or two last week. This family is not going to fall apart. Not right now." Grandma fussed.

"Okay, I am going to get on top of April." I kissed my Granny on the forehead and went directly into the other room to find April. Before I could even get the door open my phone vibrated. It was a text message from an unknown contact that read:

*"Get to the hospital NOW. Lauren is not feeling well at all!"*

Just when I thought things were looking up for us I get this message. I told gram I'd see her later and rushed out the door. "I love ya'll, I'll be back tonight I promise. Come on Bud we got to go."

When I arrived at the hospital the entire room was full of silence. All heads turned my way and their eyes pierced me. I knew right then and there that shit just got real. "Mrs. Carter what is going on?" I asked as I leaned down into Lauren's chest hoping she would hear my voice and wake up. "Son, Lauren fell into a coma. Her brain has been bleeding slowly for the past couple of days and it caused her brain to shut down." Mrs. Carter explained. I fell to my knees. There was nowhere else to go but down. I cried like a baby. "Mrs. Carter what do you mean? Why isn't this something they detected earlier on? I know they had to have seen the bleeding. I can't take this. I literally can't take this."

"'Let's give Robert a moment with Lauren. Come on you all." Mrs. Carter told the others.

"Yo, you good? Do you need my help man? Come on and get up. Sit in the chair bro. She is going to pull through it man." Bud did the best he could to give me strength but nothing would suffice at this point. I just need my girl to wake up from this.

*"Why God? Why do you let shit like this happen? It's bad enough you ain't gave me shit to begin with. I never believed the hype because I never had anything to show for it. I can't understand how I'd be born into this bullshit life. You took everything from me. Everything!"* I punched a hole straight into the wall. "Robert! You can't do this here. I understand trust me, this is my baby girl we're talking about but I can't allow you to behave like this here. Just think about Lauren right now. Go step out man. Get it together!" Mr. Carter finally spoke to me in a genuine tone. I tell Bud to follow me outside and I get into my car to take him home. Bud knew not to say much at all. We sat in silence the entire

ride. Bud gets out of the car and I speed off without saying a word. "Dammit! Lauren wanted me to come and see her today and I messed it up dealing with my sister and her drama. This shit is crazy but I know things will turnaround. They have to." I'm thinking to myself. I finally make it home and kiss my grandmother on her forehead.

"Robert, I've been worried about you lately. You have been moving around pretty fast lately. What is it son what's going on?" Grandma had her way of knowing things before I even told her. "Well gram, Lauren went into a coma and I'm just messed up over it. I'm just stuck on the fact that when I left her everything was fine with her and now all of a sudden, she's half way gone." There was a long moment of silence before grandma responded. Not sure she even knows what to say.

"I'm sorry to hear that Robert. The only thing we can do right now is pray right now. And you need to stay strong for her family. It'll be okay Robert, she will come out of it and you will get through it." Grandma said. If no one else, my grandma always got my back.

# Chapter 7

*April...*

Laid out on the couch I can feel the sunrays warming my skin a bit and the light became unbearable. I had fallen asleep right here on this couch. I grabbed the phone to call Bruce, it's early but he is a businessman, he should be awake by now. "Hello Bruce, how are you this morning?" I asked him.

"I am great now that I hear your voice. I've been thinking about you all night. I can't wait to see you later on." Bruce responded.

"That's funny because I don't think I slept very much at all. I fell asleep on the couch at god knows what time; I was really trying to finish the laundry before the night ended. Bu anyway, yes I can't wait to see you too."

"Okay beautiful, you go ahead and get our day going so we can do all of what's needed before later."

"Okay Bruce, sounds good. I'll just meet you at the train station around 4:30, you know the train ride there is about an hour." I told him.

"That's perfect. See you at 4:30."

I hang up the phone and wake Tyson and Aaliyah to get them both ready for school. The first thing Aaliyah says is, "Why are you smiling so hard April? There is definitely something going on with you."

I laughed out loud. "Girl you are too funny. Just mind your own little business. I can't be happy when I wake up in the morning? What's so wrong with that?" I told her. Aaliyah didn't say much after that. I continue getting them dressed and walk them outside to their bus stop. I reach down to kiss them both and proceed back into the house. I quickly flat iron my edges to make sure my hair is on point, turn my room upside down to find the best outfit possible, and head out the door for school. "Grandma, I'm gone! I'll be staying after school today for a project. See you later." That's it, my day has finally begun and my long boots and sweater skirt were perfect for the day. The only great thing about winter is being able to switch up your attire. There is so much variety with winter clothes. I made it to school and of course I run straight into Donnie. I did my very best at ignoring him but he tugged at my arm. "What's up April?"

"Hey, Donnie. Nothing's up."

"So that's it, nothing's up? You look nice today."

"Thanks, I really appreciate that. You look handsome also." I said, sarcastically. "Donnie, I really better get going. I don't want to be late to class."

"Aiight then. Take care of yourself." Donnie says.

I rushed into the building and took my seat. Of course the only thing on my mind is meeting Bruce tonight. I could care less about what this teacher is talking about. Every class was pretty much the same. I did just enough to get through it. In and out and before I knew it, school was out. I nearly ran out of there. Called Bruce immediately just to be sure he would be there.

I am walking to the train station with so many thoughts running through my head. It was the longest train ride ever. But after about forty-five minutes I had finally made it. As soon as I stepped foot off the train Bruce was right there holding a dozen roses. "This must really be the week of flowers…" I thought to myself. "Wow Bruce, what are you doing with all this?"

"What do you mean, these are for you?" Bruce says as he hands them to me. "Well thank you, they're beautiful. Alright what's on the agenda this evening?" I asked.

"Well, first we are headed back to my placc. I want to show you more of my world and then I have a huge surprise for you. So I'll allow you to rest and do whatever you need to do before we head to the excitement." Bruce replies.

"Sounds good!" I was happy to get my mind off my reality for a while. I can't make this man any promises, but I'll enjoy the time here and appreciate the moment. We arrive at Bruce's condo and it's immaculate. It was spotless from floor to ceiling. I couldn't believe a man living by himself actually lived like this. I had never seen anything like it. All the men I have known are all pigs. They were extremely sloppy and never really took care of much around the house. I snooped around searching for clues of him lying or maybe some evidence that he was actually someone else. How do I know his name is even really Bruce? I was digging for anything I could find. The home was very upscale with all these French pieces I'd seen only from watching T.V. The chandelier in the dining room really put the icing on the cake. It was breath taking. I finally gave up on playing detective and just as Bruce suggested, I lay down for a much needed nap. Suddenly, I hear a phone ring and it most certainly stops me from dosing off. I quickly get it together and find Bruce to be nosey and listen in on his conversation. He wasn't very far, right in his office reading some book and whispering on his phone to someone. I tried to get an idea of what he was reading, but the cover was a plain brown color no words, no photo. This guy is just plain weird, but I like it. I busted right in on him, "okay Bruce, what's the plan?"

"We're headed out of town. Do you have your I.D.? If not, it's not a big deal we'll be flying on my private jet. Since you don't have clothes we can shop once we get there."

"Bruce, are you crazy? A private jet? How? I need to know where we're going, where we'll be staying and when we'll be coming back." I didn't tell Bruce my age yet but he seems to be much older than I am obviously. So I really didn't want to show him my I.D.

"We're going to Los Angeles where it's warm and sunny. Bruce laughed. We'll only be gone for a day. I have to work and I figured I'd bring you along since you say you've never been and let you see something new."

"Wow! I am speechless, but excited! I need to make a phone call first. Can I use your phone?" I asked.

I grab Bruce's phone and call Destiny on her cell. I explained everything and she was beyond excited but nervous at the same time. I just called her so that at least she had his phone number and name and so that she could give me a call tomorrow on the number if she hadn't heard from me by then. I am excited to go sightseeing, but I'm extremely nervous. "What am I thinking?" I thought to myself. "He was truly a peculiar guy." It is most definitely time for me to start asking Mr. Jackson some questions. "So Bruce, how old are you? And were you born in West Chester? Where is your family, are they here also?"

"Whoa, whoa, please slow down miss beauty queen, one at a time." He pleaded.

"I just want to know everything, you're so different. And why were you on the train today if you have a private jet?"

"Different, what do you mean different? I hate it when people insist and try labeling me into some outrageous category. Why does it matter that I fit into one of your boxes?" Bruce exclaimed.

"Well, I don't want to box you in but Bruce you're such an amazing person, I just wanted to know how you got here. You are very unique, but I never said anything was wrong with it." I explained to Bruce. He began telling me his life story and before we knew it, we were right in front of the airport. Bruce cut it short and we got out of the car and were escorted straight into the airport past security and everything. It took no time for us to get onto the plane. A few others joined us and Bruce introduced me to them as his new friend. Everyone was very pleasant but the entire plane ride was business for Bruce. We didn't talk much at all. Every now and then he leaned over and asked me if I was okay. And of course I made sure he didn't have to worry about me at all. He already had enough going on. As I looked out of the window, I couldn't help but think about myself and my own future. I had never been on a plane before and what an amazing sight it is. I was fortunate to have had the experience, even if I never got the chance to do it again. I vowed to myself to put my troubles aside and enjoy this trip.

### 4 hours later…

I felt a nudge on my knee, "prepare for landing." The flight attendant said. I excitedly put my seat belt on and stuffed my bag underneath the seat. The sun was beaming; I was in pure bliss. Los Angeles is the most beautiful place ever. Bruce took my hand and kissed it. That was the solidification I needed. I instantly felt safe.

We got to the front of the airport and a Lincoln was waiting for us. A tall chocolate man opened my door and took my hand to assist me into the car. Bruce's "*entourage*" followed behind us in another car. I immediately turn to Bruce and kissed him on the cheek and thanked him for inviting me. "You're so welcome honey. The moment I laid eyes on you, I knew you needed me in your life." Bruce said with confidence.

"You sound so sure, Mr. Jackson. What makes you so sure I needed you?" I ask.

"Oh, you'll see babe, just wait." He says.

As I'm looking out the window, I was just in awe ...

**Dear Journal,**

*We finally made it Los Angeles, I never imagined myself here but here I am. The palm trees are just as beautiful as they are on T.V. I'm in love with this place already. After all I've been through in the last couple of months I would have never guessed I'd be with someone like Bruce. Bruce is starting to open up to me and involving me more into his personal and business affairs. The mess between Donnie and I had me really depressed for a while but Bruce was just as patient as he was the first day I met him. Honestly, I'm still not as in love with Bruce as I was Donnie. Donnie was my first, I was pregnant with his baby and he* understood *a part of me that I really don't think Bruce will ever understand. Bruce came from a pretty stable background so while he was great at listening, he can't relate to how I feel most of the time. All Bruce knows to do is what he's doing right now and that's showing me new things and loving me with his money.*

# Chapter 8

We rode all around Los Angeles last night. We're staying at the Sofitel in Beverly Hills. This morning I went shopping on Rodeo Dr. while Bruce was working at the studio on his new movie. Rodeo was way too upscale for me; I'm still in shock over all this. But my hair was flowing and I was wearing a sundress in the winter, I can't complain one bit. I shopped until I couldn't anymore. I bought bags, dresses, sunglasses and of course shoes. Christian Louboutin's, Gianvito Rossi's, Valentino's, and Saint Laurent's. I've always been a shoe fanatic, not ever thinking I'd ever actually be able to afford them. One o'clock came around way too fast. It was time for me to meet back up with Bruce. I made a quick call home to my grand mother; I figured she was looking all around town for me by now. "Grandma, Hey, I'm here with Destiny, we stayed up all night working on our final project. I'm so sorry. We're just going to go straight from school from here since we are already late." I was praying she'd stay calm. "April, don't ever do this again. I was worried sick about you and no one knew anything about your whereabouts. You can't do things like this April. Just one phone call will save my troubles." Grandmother continued. She went on and on about being safe and reminded me that we don't have anyone else and if she looses us how devastated she would be. She was so insecure about loosing Robert and I the way she lost my mother and Mike. Mike is on his last leg right now, and that situation is bitter sweet. Mike is a apart of our family but he was such a bad person. It was really hard to feel any remorse for him. "Okay Gram, I really need to hurry and I am so sorry about this. I love you." I pleaded.

The Lincoln was right outside waiting for me and I got right in. I finally made it to Bruce and he hopped in and greeted me with a kiss. "How was your day baby girl?" Bruce asked.

"It was great. The trunk speaks volumes." I laughed.

"I'm glad you enjoyed it." He replied.

"This was the best day ever Bruce." We headed back to the hotel room. My assumption was that we were about to get ready to pack up and head back to the airport but as I opened our door there were rose pedals everywhere. "WOW! What is all this?" The bellman carried my shopping bags inside and quietly left as Bruce tipped him and continued inside the room. April, I told you you were everything. Very beautiful and exquisite, one of the classiest women I've ever met. Your beauty captivates me from the day I laid my eyes on you. I wanted to ask you if you would take me hand and become a part of my family as my 'lady'. I want you to be my woman. I literally had no words. I couldn't hold back my smile. "Yes of course." I replied to him. I'd love to take on that position in your life.

### Dear Journal

*I've seen this play out before. This feels like a movie. Sometimes these situations end well but on the flip side, when they don't they really don't. In fact, they end terribly. I liked Bruce, but no way am I in love with him the way I was in love with Donnie. Honestly, a part of me is still in love with Donnie. What can I say, we spent years together, before any intimacy, we were good friends. So I am still having trust issues right now. But I couldn't tell that to Bruce. He was spending all this money on me and he seems so serious about asking me to be his girl. If I turned him down, he'd be devastated. Besides, all these things and random trips is something I can get used to. Maybe I'd grow to love him at some point. But for now, I'll play the role. Since that's what these men do anyway. They just play the role to get what they want. They tell us any ole lie just to get by. They reel us in, get us all caught up into them while they still do any and everything. It's about time I live for me.*

Right after accepted Bruce's offer of being his leading lady, we kissed. Finally we shared a real kiss. He literally licked my neck down to my lower stomach. His passion in the bedroom was just as he displayed it outside of the bed. He was a true giver. I laid there and let him give. We slept for hours afterwards. It took his assistant to call him about five times before we finally woke up. We were running late for our plane so we rushed and gathered our things, called the car to meet us downstairs and checked out of our room.

I graduated High School just as planned. In fact I was so head over heels for Bruce that I finished a little early just so I could be with him more frequently. He demanded so much of my time. He wanted me around as often as possible. Sucked that I couldn't even invite him to my graduation. I was just glad to not have that situation hanging over my shoulders anymore. And even more excited that this day had finally come. My graduation day had given me the most bittersweet feeling. I was emotional about the fact that everyone's parents were here celebrating their children, for me on the other hand, just my Grandmother, Robert and the kids. Not that their love isn't good enough because I love my support system. Without my Grandmother, God knows where I'd be right now. Just as my thoughts cleared my head, in stumbles some strange old black man. Everyone literally stopped and starred. He looks drunk and by the looks on everyone's faces he must smell really bad. Before I knew it, the old man was screaming my name, "APRIL!!" I ducked my head underneath the chair, full of embarrassment. "What in the world is going on?" I whispered to my classmate. She tapped my shoulder and pointed out to the audience. It was my brother Robert talking with the old guy. Robert seemed really upset too. Before I blinked, Robert punched the man right in his gut. "Oh my gosh, this has to be the most ridiculous things I've ever seen. And it's just my luck. Of course this would happen to me." I blurted. After the ceremony I met up with Robert to figure out who that crazy man was. "Don't worry about that right now April, let's get some pictures taken. Enjoy the moment." Robert replied.

"No, I want to know who that man was Robert. I'm not some lil' girl anymore, stop hiding things. That's the problem. Ya'll like to sugar coat things instead of keeping it real!" I yelled.

"Okay April! You really wanna know the truth? Do you really want to know the truth?" Robert yelled back at me.

"Yes!"

"Well the truth is, that was your father. Our father, Frank!" He said.

"Are you serious? And you just punched him and sent him off Robert? Why did you do that?" I pleaded.

"Well, he was drunk and being an ass. I didn't want him ruining your day."

"But he came here for me and I didn't get to see him at all. I'm just shocked that he even made it here." My eyes began to water. "Wow, who would have thought he would actually show up? And how did he find out about it in the first place?" I questioned."

My father showing up to my graduation had really shifted the mood for the day. I did realize that I needed to continue to keep a celebratory attitude therefore I brushed it off for the remainder of the day. My family and I decided to go out to dinner that evening. We rarely do this but my grandmother really wanted to show me in her own regards, how proud she was. I think somewhere in the back of her mind she wondered if I was actually going to get it done.

After a long but productive day, I knew I needed to call Bruce he's probably worried because we talk at least two to three times a day when we're not together. I scurried to the kitchen grabbed the phone and dialed his number. Bruce answered right away. "Hey beautiful. Where have you been all my life? I was wondering when you were going to call me. I really need to go ahead and get you your own permanent line." "Hey Bruce, I know. I'm sorry I was out all day with my family. We had a graduation to go to and then dinner." I said.

"Oh okay. Who graduated?" Bruce asked.

"Um… Aaliyah graduated she's a big girl now." I laughed in hope of deflecting the convo."

"Okay that's nice then. So when am I going to see you? I want to see you right now." Bruce demanded.

"Um… Right now?"

"Yes, right now. Meet me at the station." He said.

I couldn't turn him down. But I know for a fact my grandmother isn't going to allow it so I guess I'll sneak out. Besides, I've graduated. I'm grown now.

"Okay Bruce, I'll be there in a hour." I responded.

I made sure the house was sleeping. Everyone was pooped from the day's events and Robert is of course nowhere to be found. I don't even think he lives with us anymore. That boy never sleeps here. I gathered my things and made sure I had my journal. I have so many thoughts spinning through my head right now. I nearly jogged to the station. It was dark outside and I was in the hood. I never go out at night. It's creepy and my grandmother always told me that only bad things happen outside past ten. The train was pretty much empty. I was just me and this little old lady and what seemed to be her grandkid sleeping. They looked a little run down. I was thinking about their condition as I observed them for a while. It looked like they may have been homeless. And then I thought to myself. "That could have been me. Momma is crazy as all hell. She loved drugs more than she loved me. That woman would have left me for the wolves. I'd be out here trying to find my next meal if it weren't for my grandmother. Imagine me trying to have a child. I have no clue what it's like to be someone's mother. Don't you have to actually learn how to do it, like perhaps form your mom? It saddens me to watch the mother's who actually try really hard and to know how mine just gave up."

## Dear Journal

*I question so much about my life. I love God because I truly believe I wouldn't be here if it was not for him. But I also question the parents that he has chosen for me. Today I graduated and my dad that I honestly can't remember ever seeing, showed up to my graduation. Robert kind of knew Frank. My mother used to share stories about Frank to my big brother. So at least he has some idea of what he might be like. But me, I know nothing. I had no way of knowing that that was him today. He showed up drunk so I guess that sort of explains why we never see him around. In some weird way it gave me some kind of joy to see that he at least showed up. But I'm still heartbroken from not ever having him in my life. I mean all the shit I dealt with growing up between Uncle Mike and his friends and my mother pretty much selling me to her crack friends, I was humiliated as a child. Would have been nice to have someone there to protect me. Like this one night, I had to be about nine going on ten because I remember talking about my birthday coming up. This was before Robert and I stayed with my grandmother, I was sleep in my room and I heard three soft knocks on my window. I never really fell into a deep sleep back then because most nights I was half awake wondering when my mother was coming home. I recognized the face as one of my mom's friends so I opened my window to see if maybe he had information on her whereabouts. "Where is my mom?" I asked.*

*"She aint in my damn pocket. Just let me in." He replied.*

*Being naïve I opened the window for him. My mother had an open house. She always allowed people to come and stay with us if they didn't have a place to sleep. I threw him a blanket and pillow and went back into my bed. Well, before I could even close my eyes, I felt a hand rising up my gown. I screamed to the top of my lungs. Luckily Robert was there and rushed in. He wrestled with the guy and kicked him out.*

*Robert wasn't that old at that time but he did what he could to keep me safe.*

The train came to a complete stop. I had finally made it to Bruce. He was waiting right in the front of the station parked in his BMW 650i. I couldn't help but wonder if that lady and child had a place to go. So I asked them if I could help them get somewhere and the woman's eye's got really big and she told me they had no where to go. I immediately tell Bruce about them to see if he could help. He handed me five hundred dollar bills and I gladly gave it to the lady. She fell to her knees and cried. Told me I was an angel. I felt good I could be a part of helping that woman.

Bruce greeted me with a French kiss this time. "Whoa, someone's in a good mood." I told him.

"Yes, I am actually. It's good to see you. Missed those bright brown eyes. You're such a sweet person to pay attention to others like that. I knew there was something about you that I loved." He told me.

"Well I'm glad you're in a good mood Bruce."

"Are you hungry? He asked.

"No, we went to dinner. I can do a snack or something light but other than that, I'm fine."

"Okay, let's get home then."

"Home, as in your home, right?"

"My home is your home." Bruce responded.

"Oh, okay then." I couldn't help but smile. Bruce always did me like this.

"Yeah I've been meaning to ask you, when are you going to go ahead and move in?" He stated.

"Well, I didn't know that was an option sir. I guess I can think about it." I told him.

"Think about it? What is there to think about?" Bruce said with aggression. He also gets so confrontational when I said things he didn't want to hear. I realized that about him.

"Can we just enjoy the night Bruce? Of course I want to move in but I need to clear things with my family first. My grandmother isn't getting any older and she still has Aaliyah and Tyson there. Robert is never at home and kind of going through something himself right now. I don't want to just up and leave them." I had to really break it down for his ass. He just doesn't get it. He told me that he'd help my grandmother with any money she needed to take care of the kids and that I could still go over there from time to time to help out. We talked about it the entire ride home. I was good with thinking about it but there is no way I'm giving him an answer right away.

# Chapter 9

Bruce had two glasses of wine sitting on his breakfast bar as waiting for us as we walked through the door. It was fascinating to me the way he'd always have something waiting for me every single time we got together. "Are you going to be this way when I move in too?" I asked him.

"Be like what?" He questioned.

"Like this, the surprises and stuff."

"Of course, I'll never change. I told you already. You are my virtue. I get peace when I'm around you."

"This man is crazy I thought to myself." I just can't get over the fact that he always said the 'right things'. We sat there and shared silence while finishing our glasses. Bruce grabbed his remote and before I knew it there was some slow classical music he had playing. He went into the bathroom and came back with a bottle, grabbed my foot and squirted oils all over it. He began to massage my foot and then my leg and then moved up to my thigh. That landed us in his bedroom. He was a straight professional at this thing. I knew right then and there that I had become sprung. I was high off his attention. He was giving me what I needed emotionally and physically. I slept right there in his arms.

**

Now that it was spring, heading into summer, you couldn't dare sleep pass seven thirty. Bruce has a very large window in his bedroom and the sun literally smacked you in the face in the morning. I got up and showed Bruce a little bit of my cooking skills. I made us two stuffed omelets and poured him a glass of orange juice. Bruce loved my efforts.

"Unfortunately, I need to get back to check on Grandmother and the kids." I told him.

"When can I meet them?" He asked.

"I guess you can meet them soon. I don't see a problem with that. I'm sure my Grandma will love you."

"One more thing before we head out." Bruce walked into his closet and brings out this huge box. "Open it." He said.

I opened the box to find another beautiful sundress and the latest Gucci gg supreme canvas summer edition. "This is perfect!" I screamed and hopped right into his arms.

"We're spending the day together so come on so you can hurry up and take care of things at your Grandmother's house real quick." Bruce was so demanding but I must admit that I kind of enjoyed that about him. On our way back North to my neighborhood, Bruce made a stop at this little mom and popshop. I sat there and waited for him to come out for about thirty minutes. On his way out there was some lady screaming his name and throwing papers at him. Bruce hurried into the car and we were finally on the highway headed to my grandmother's house. I didn't even bother to ask Bruce about whom the woman was, I figured I'd deal with that issue later on. Bruce came over to my side of the car and opened the door for me. We both headed to the front door and I used my key to get in. I guess Bruce might as well meet my Gma, I was technically grown and able to make my own decisions now. I will just make this short and sweet. As soon as I hit the door with Bruce, Aaliyah is the first one to say something. "Who is this man, April?"

"This man's name is Bruce, Bruce Jackson." I replied. "He's a very nice man at that.

"Hello Aaliyah, it's a pleasure meeting you." Bruce reached his hand out for hers.

"Hi Bruce. I hope you're a nice person like April says. This is my best cousin." Aaliyah gave Bruce the run down. Meanwhile I went into my grandmother's bedroom to explain to her that I had company here for her to meet. She popped right out of her chair and washed her face. "Why didn't you call first April?" She complained.

Grandmother smiled at Bruce and greeted him. Bruce reached for her hand and kissed it. "It's a pleasure to have met the person responsible for this classy lady you have here." Bruce told her. I can tell that she is pleased with the kind of man Bruce was. He used the same charm on her that he used to catch me. Before Bruce could start asking too many questions I explained to her that he had travel plans in the evening so we had to get going. Bruce would have sat there all day if I had let him. Grandma walked us to the door and hugged me tight. She hugged me and had a look in her eyes as if it was her last time seeing me. I kissed her and told her I loved her. There is just something about a grandmother's love that'll never be replaced. Just before I got into the car I see Donnie from the corner of my eye. Trying to hurry the situation, I told Bruce to come on and stop talking so much. "April!" It was too late. "Shit!" I thought to myself.

"Yo April." Donnie yelled again.

"Hey, Donnie." I replied. I had no other choice. Bruce started looking at Donnie and me suspiciously; I went ahead and introduced the two of them. "This is Bruce, Bruce this is Donnie." Neither of them spoke to one another. I was able to break the silence with explain to Donnie, I'd be gone and prompted him to check on my Grandmother from time to time. He was cool with that and Bruce and I proceeded on. As soon as we pulled Bruce grabbed my wrist and questioned me about Donnie. "Who the hell was that?"

"That's just a childhood friend so please let go of me" I yelled. "What the fuck you mean a childhood friend. I saw the way he looked at you. That was not the way a friend looks at another friend."

"Yes, it is just a friend Bruce, what are you talking about? He didn't look at me any kind of way. You are really trippin' and can you please let me go."

"Naw, I'm not letting shit go. You can play these games if you want to April, but you'll find out real fast that I'm not the one." He grabbed my wrist even harder.

"Are you crazy? This is far from anything I'd ever expect from you. This is some bullshit."

"No, what's bullshit is you thinking it's okay to keep things from me." He finally threw my hand down and keep driving.

"Damn Bruce, all this over just some little boy off the block. I can just imagine what you'll be like when I actually get some real attention." Bruce slammed onto the brakes and smacked me until I blacked completely out.

**(Meanwhile)**

*Robert …*

After speaking with my Grandmother, I figured I may as well stay strong for Lauren's family and do whatever it is they couldn't stomach enough courage to do themselves. I mean I've seen a lot of things in my lifetime but one thing I've actually never dealt with is this. Having someone I love and care about in a coma. It's this awkward place in-between life and death. I ran errands for Mrs. Carter, I mowed their lawn, I did just about everything they asked. It's been a while and Lauren's condition is still stabilized but she has not woke up yet. I did start going to church with Gram recently thought since April wasn't around like that anymore. I spent most of my nights at the Carter's anyway so it was the least I could do. I still did what I had to do in the streets and what not but I made sure even if it was only five minutes that I made to see Lauren before each day ended.

As I walked through the double doors of the hospital I could hear loud screams coming from the back area where Lauren's family hung out. I couldn't tell if they were screams of joys or sadness, nonetheless I hurried. I ran right pass the front desk but by now I figured they knew me enough not to call the security guards. As soon as I stepped foot in the waiting area, Mrs. Carter hugged me as tight as she could. Even Mr. Carter joined in. I was still at a lost because no one was saying a word. So I just stood there. Allowing the hugs because the last thing I want to hear about is something bad right now. I've had enough bad in my life.

**

*April …*

Bruce and I had finally made it home. That was probably the most violent I had seen him. I went into the bathroom and cared for my hand that felt like it was about to fall off. All the while I was thinking about the fact that Bruce never did explain to me who that was he was arguing with at that little store we stopped by earlier. He was so insecure about Donnie, but what about that woman. At least I had reason to believe there had been something going on between him and her. Bruce on the other hand is basing he assumptions off a look that supposedly Donnie gave me. I brushed it off and didn't worry about it much more. Bruce came right over and kissed my forehead. When he did that it literally made my heart melt. I immediately felt safe again. Just his scent alone has me so hooked.

"Come one baby we're going to the movies. I still want us to enjoy the evening as planned." He told me.

"Okay, me too babe." "Let's make it old school and take the train up there. It's nothing but a couple train stops up but I think you'll enjoy the light walk." He suggested.

"Sounds good to me." We walked hand and hand. He was never afraid of letting the world know I was his lady. I guess he wanted me to do the same.

"April, I'm sorry about earlier. I shouldn't have gotten so upset. It's just that I have a shaky past when it comes to women. So I get very uncomfortable in situations like that. Next time you need to introduce me as your man. I think that'll help the situation to never happen again."

As he explained more I kind of started to understand a bit more of why Bruce was the way he was. Yet, I was still curious about the girl from earlier. Since we're in such a good space right now, he shouldn't have a problem at all answering any of my questions. I'm going to ask about it right after our movie. Just as Bruce wanted our walk and train ride were relaxing. We paid one another undivided attention. Before I could get another word out, I heard a squeaky voice from the other side of the train.

"Bruce …!" The voice got closer and closer to us. Until I finally asked him, "Who is that Bruce? Who is that yelling your name?" I asked.

Bruce was being very protective. I was really getting nervous now, I thought to myself, "what in the world is going on?" Once we got out of the off the train Bruce grabbed my hand and pulled me so fast, I didn't get the chance to even think about it. Before I knew it we had made it to the theater. Bruce pulled me into his chest and there it goes again, that feeling, this man is everything. Yet I still need answers, "So who was that Mr. Jackson? "Should I be heading back home now? It's a lot going on out here right now." "NO!" He yelled. "You're not going anywhere girl, you are staying with me. You'll go home when I say you're going and even then, I'm going with you."

"What … what do you mean? You're scaring me." I was slightly afraid but still attracted to the way it seemed Bruce cared for me. I've never had anyone want me the way he was showing me he wanted me. He then took a deep breath and spoke quietly, "Calm down beautiful, I'm just saying that I need to make sure you get home safely. And by home I mean, my condo that we are now sharing, I'm just that way, I want to be sure that you're okay."

"Oh." I said. He never did answer my question about who that was pretty much stalking us the whole day. But I ignored it because now I am afraid of what this man is up to. The most I can do is keep him calm and try getting away.
"BRUUUUCE!"

"Are you kidding me? What the hell is going on?" Now I'm just getting fed up with the whole situation. I wasn't sure what was about to unfold but I was for certain something was going to happen.

"We have to get out of here." Bruce said. "Let's go!"

Once we made it back to his condo I ran straight into the bathroom.

***Dear Journal***

*Remember that beautiful stranger I was telling you about? Well I think he has so much more to hide than I thought. I think this guy is psychotic for real. But I am oh so attracted to his craziness. I just want to be with him. He takes good care of me. I know I made my mistake with Donnie and all but Bruce was older, more mature. He knows exactly what to do with me. On the flip side, he has definitely shown me he has an anger problem and he is very possessive. I think somewhere in that little head of his he thinks I'm staying here forever. I just can't deal with more heartbreak. Bruce was everything I needed and more. But I really need to find out who this person is following him. But tonight is going to be epic; I am going to demand that Bruce tell me who that person is. I am not sure how he'll respond but it's worth a try.*

I walked out of the bathroom and heard Bruce calling me from his bedroom. I made my way over and he has candles lit and the fireplace burning. I must admit I'm really into this romantic chivalry stuff Bruce has introduced me to. This man sure does know how to reel you in. I know exactly what he's up to and I refuse to go there this time. There is no way he's going to ignore the situation. Bruce said to me, "why are you still standing there girl, get over here." I gave in a little bit and walked over to him. He sat me down on his lap. Bruce lifted my shirt and he started at my neck and worked his fingers down my spine and into my love handles. My blood was rushing and I think my heart is about to burst through my chest from all this adrenaline. Bruce then slowly pulled my pants down to my knees and I couldn't help but gasp for air. He went straight for the gold. Just as Bruce began taking his clothes completely off, I stopped him in his tracks, "I, I can't do this."

"You can't do what April? What is the problem?"

"Who was that crazy woman following us today Bruce?" I inquired. Bruce then lifted his hand and the look in his eyes was a look that was all too familiar. Bruce slapped me across my face and called me out my name. It was the ultimate disrespect. I was beyond embarrassed and full of guilt. This has happened much too frequently today and now I felt ugly. His entire hand was imprinted on my cheek. I didn't cry because I was sort of used to stuff like this. I gathered myself together and ran into the bathroom. While trying to clear my face I heard a loud knock at the front door. "Who is that and why didn't they use the bell." I thought out loud. Bruce ran down the stairs and all I hear is him telling someone to leave him alone and that he wants nothing to do with the person. I rushed out of the bathroom to quickly head to the front door to see what was going on. A woman busted through the door screaming at Bruce, "You did this to me. You told me you loved me and here I am stuck in this crazy ass triangle. I need you to do something Bruce, and who the hell is this little chick you have in here? Is this some kind of game you always play Bruce? Is it Bruce?"

"Tanya, I'm sorry. I didn't want you to catch those kinds of feelings. But I can't keep going through this with you. You need to go back to your husband and care for your family. What we did was a complete mistake Tanya," Bruce pleaded.

"But Bruce I need you. You can't just do this. I left my husband and he wants nothing to do with me now."

I need for you to leave my house and go home before I call the police. I really don't want to have to go there with you but I will." Bruce continued.

"Who is this little ass girl you have here Bruce, call the police… hell I'll call the police and let them know you over here messing with little ass kids." Tanya was pissed.

"You have no idea what's going on here, so you need to leave. Who I have in my home is none of your business at all." Bruce finally pushed Tanya out the door. But as she left she still screamed, "I will find out what's going on here Bruce, so you'd better clean up this mess."

Once Bruce finally shut the door, his eyes were red and he was clearly raging like a bull! "Why the hell did you come out of the bathroom? I thought you were much smarter than that, so stupid of you April." Bruce kept fussing for at least another thirty minutes. I let him ramble as he slowly calmed down. I didn't say anything back to him at all.

 "You can have this room tonight." He said. The only thing I can do at this point is agree with Bruce and go to bed.

**

As the sun peeks, I feel the rays on my back. The bed sat right in front of the large window in the room. I looked over to the clock to see what time it was and it was nine o'clock. I pulled my journal out and begin writing:

*Bruce made our night epic just as expected. After demanding the truth from him he slapped me across my face. I still have the imprint and my face is still red. Only if Bruce knew just how familiar all this was to me. My uncle Mike was infatuated with me for years. From age 10 up until I turned about 15 when he got sick. Is it terrible that I was happy as hell when Mike got cancer? I was freed from his chains. The man had me on a tight leash and no one even noticed. Shows you how screwed up my family really is. Anyway, I can't figure out whether or not Bruce hates me now or if he'll just become more possessive. This is turning into some weird beautiful nightmare. The rage in Bruce's eyes was something I would have never expected from him when we first met. And how about this crazy woman chasing us all night and then banging on his door?? She was hysterical. But I guess I'm the idiot for putting my hopes in a beautiful stranger. I'll continue this later; I'm sure Bruce's psychotic self is sniffing around and knows that I'm awake by now.*

I closed my journal and stuffed it in my backpack. Surely enough, Bruce busted straight through the doors.

25744605R00080

Made in the USA
Middletown, DE
09 November 2015